INDIAN IMMIGRANTS
IN THEIR SHOES

BY JEANNE MARIE FORD

Published by The Child's World®
1980 Lookout Drive • Mankato, MN 56003-1705
800-599-READ • www.childsworld.com

Content Consultant: Ronak D. Desai, Affiliate, India and South Asia Program, Harvard
Kennedy School

Photographs ©: Kike Calvo/AP Images, cover, 1; Shutterstock Images, 6, 8; Everett
Historical/Shutterstock Images, 9; Picture History/Newscom, 10; iStockphoto, 12;
Andrew Shurtleff/The Daily Progress/AP Images, 14; Charles Rex Arbogast/AP
Images, 15; Tarapong Srichaiyos/Shutterstock Images, 16; Rahul Ramachandram/
Shutterstock Images, 18; John Raoux/AP Images, 20; Fred Zwicky/Journal Star/AP
Images, 21; Paul Sakuma/AP Images, 22; Dragon Images/Shutterstock Images, 24;
Rawpixel.com/Shutterstock Images, 25; India Picture/Shutterstock Images, 26; Red
Line Editorial, 28

ISBN 9781503827981
LCCN 2018944220

Printed in the United States of America
PA02394

ABOUT THE AUTHOR

Jeanne Marie Ford is an Emmy-winning TV scriptwriter who holds a master of
fine arts degree in writing for children from Vermont College. She has written
numerous children's books and articles. Ford also teaches college English.
She lives in Maryland with her husband and two children.

TABLE OF CONTENTS

FAST FACTS

Facts about India

- India is a country in South Asia. It has the second-largest population in the world.

- People in India speak many languages. The most common languages include Hindi, English, Bengali, and Tamil.

- The majority of Indian people practice Hinduism. Other major religions include Buddhism, Islam, Sikhism, and Christianity.

- For hundreds of years, the **caste** system separated Indian society into strict social classes.

Waves of Indian Immigration

- The first major wave of Indian immigrants came to the United States after the 1965 Hart-Celler Act. This act increased immigration from the East. It gave priority to highly skilled and educated immigrants.

- The second wave of Indian immigration came in the 1980s. The third wave of immigration began with the technology boom of the late 1990s. The third wave consisted mainly of skilled workers and their families.

4

TIMELINE

1917: The Immigration Act of 1917 bans most Asian immigrants.

1946: The Luce-Celler Act allows a limited number of Indians to apply for U.S. citizenship.

1965: The Hart-Celler Act is passed. The number of Indian immigrants to the United States increases significantly.

1965–1980: The first wave of Indian immigrants begins to arrive in the United States.

1980s: The second wave of Indian immigrants begins. These immigrants join family members who arrived during the first wave of immigration.

1990: The Immigration Act of 1990 allows more permanent work **visas** for skilled workers from overseas.

Late 1990s: The third and largest wave of Indian immigrants begins arriving in the United States.

Chapter 1

THE PIONEERS

On August 25, 1949, Roshan Sharma climbed on shaky legs to the ship's deck. Life aboard the ship was difficult. For weeks he'd eaten a lot of boiled rice and potatoes. Like many Indians, Sharma was a vegetarian. The whole fish he was served at almost every meal rolled his stomach.

Now the United States' shoreline stretched before him in the distance. San Francisco's Golden Gate Bridge glinted against the blue sky.

Sharma knew from listening to American radio that many immigrant hands had built the bridge. He thought it looked like "a real gateway to . . . heaven on earth."[1]

The passengers formed snaking lines as they left the ship. A friendly American bought Sharma a sandwich. Only after Sharma had gobbled it hungrily did he learn that it was a beef hamburger. Sharma's Hindu faith held that cows should be respected. Sharma wondered how something he'd been taught not to eat could taste so good.

A few weeks later, he enrolled in college classes at the University of California, Los Angeles. There were not many Indian students. One day, Sharma saw a young woman walk by in traditional Indian dress. He thought she was beautiful. Sharma summoned his courage, threw his lunch aside, and approached her. He boldly asked the young woman out on a date. The woman smiled at him and agreed. Nine months later, they were married.

Indian immigrants attending college in the United States often felt they didn't fully belong in either culture. Everyday interactions could be confusing. They'd learned British English in school in India. However, they often spoke with heavy accents, and American slang could be unfamiliar.

▲ **There are many Hindu temples in the United States. This one is in Chicago, Illinois.**

Some Indian immigrants moved to the **segregated** South. B. P. Rao attended college in Virginia in the early 1960s. He was shocked to find restrooms for blacks and whites. He paused, not sure which one he should enter. He chose the white restroom. Everyone stared at him. He left quickly. In a restaurant, a server refused to wait on him and his friends. Instead, they bought cheese and crackers at the grocery store and ate them in the car.

While many people were kind to Rao, sometimes he felt unwelcome in the United States. In 1960, only about 12,000 Indian immigrants lived in the country. Many were children and grandchildren of Sikhs who had come to the United States.

▲ People of color in the South were treated unfairly during segregation. Many public areas were divided into separate sections for white people and people of color.

▲ **President Calvin Coolidge signed the Immigration Act of 1924. This act barred Asians from moving to the United States.**

These Sikhs had arrived in the early 1900s to work on farms and railroads on the West Coast. They often received lower wages than white workers. Many faced intense **discrimination**.

The United States Immigration Commission said in 1911 that South Asians were "the least desirable race of immigrants thus far admitted to the United States."[2] Laws passed in the early 1900s barred nearly all Asians from becoming U.S. citizens or from even entering the country. In 1946, the United States began admitting Indian immigrants again. Many, such as Sharma and Rao, came to the United States to attend college. However, a **quota** system allowed only about 100 Indians to enter per year. When the quota was finally lifted in 1965, that number would increase dramatically.

"I decided to go to the U.S. to study so that I could get a better education and earn more money for my family. One of my uncles went to London to study, and sent us back gifts and letters describing how great life was in England. That motivated me to go abroad so that I could lead a better life and earn more money. I was one of the oldest sons and I had eleven other siblings to support, along with my mom."[3]

—B. P. Rao

11

Chapter 2

FIRST WAVE OF INDIAN IMMIGRANTS

Basil Varkey knew he would need a winter coat when moving from tropical South India to frigid Wisconsin to work as a doctor. From his pocket, Varkey pulled out a photograph of the coat he wanted. He handed it to his town's tailor. The tailor stared at the image before nodding to Varkey. He did his best to copy the design. Gloves were another story.

The only ones Varkey could find were made of silk and used for funeral rituals.

In late 1965, Varkey's plane landed at the Milwaukee, Wisconsin, airport. His flight was several hours late. He scanned the crowd for the doctor who was supposed to meet him, but he'd already left. "I was in a strange land of white giants," Varkey said.[4] He stepped outside and braced himself against the wind. For the first time in his life, he saw fluffy snowflakes floating down from the sky.

Varkey walked to a pay phone. He tried putting different U.S. coins in the slot until he found the one that fit. It felt like solving a puzzle. Finally, he reached the hospital administrator, who sent a taxi to fetch him.

"No voices of dear ones, no crows cawing, no stunning greens of coconut trees and bushes and no pleasing smell of jasmine flowers. The reality hit me: I am far away from home."[5]

—*Basil Varkey, MD*

One of Varkey's first stops at the hospital was the cafeteria. Unfamiliar foods lay before him and he didn't like many of them.

13

▲ **Some doctors come to the United States because there is advanced medical technology.**

Salt and pepper did not help make the bland meat and potatoes more appealing. Only the chocolate milk tasted good.

Varkey met the other medical professionals he would be working with. All of them were from other countries, but he was the only one from India. A sense of loneliness washed over him as he tried to write a cheerful letter home.

Some Indian immigrants come to the United States for ▶ medical school.

▲ **Turmeric can be used to help people's stomach problems.**

Varkey was among the first Indian doctors, engineers, and scientists who came to the United States after the 1965 Hart-Celler Act. This law made changes to the U.S. immigration system. It increased the number of immigrants admitted from Asia. It also gave priority to people with specific skills or advanced education. Today, one in 20 U.S. doctors is Indian American.

About 12,000 Indians, nearly all of them men, came to the United States each year following the passage of the new law. Among them was 23-year-old Mafat Patel, who came to study engineering at Indiana University in 1968. After graduating with a master's degree, he found work in Chicago, Illinois. Although a community of Indian American men was slowly growing around him, he missed his family terribly. He missed the aromas and foods of his childhood. In the United States, he couldn't even find the spices he needed to cook his favorite meals.

When Patel and his friends visited India, they came back to the United States with canisters of rice flour and **turmeric** tucked into their luggage. Patel decided to open a grocery store that would make these ingredients available to Indian immigrants. Familiar food helped the United States feel more like home.

"My appetite for the foods I could find inside Patel Brothers became bottomless in that period. . . . I craved chana chor, a spiced, fried chickpea snack that my parents and I mixed with Rice Krispies and had during tea in the afternoon."[6]

—Mayukh Sen, an Indian American writer

Chapter 3

FAMILY

Sakti Kunz smoothed the wrinkles from her best silk **sari** as she fidgeted in her airplane seat. She had never traveled on a plane before. She had met her new groom only once—at their wedding. He lived in the United States, and now she would, too.

It was February 1983. The streets of New York were covered in snow. Kunz had always imagined snow would be beautiful and white. Now she shuffled through grayish black mounds of city slush.

She wore her new sandals and her toes were freezing. The hem of her sari was dripping wet. "But this is America," she reassured herself. "How can it be bad?"[7]

Kunz was among the second major wave of Indian immigrants. Like her, most immigrants came to join family members in the United States. Many had heard stories that made the country sound like a fairy tale. However, reality would be more complicated.

Humaira Basith moved to Illinois when he was six years old. His uncle had been the first member of his extended family to come to the United States. Every relative who followed crammed into his uncle's home for several months while getting accustomed to American life. The newcomers had to learn how to shop at grocery stores and operate unfamiliar appliances.

> "With time, the homesickness becomes less intense, but it's been 25 years and I still feel it at times. My heart resides in two different countries, and I love each one for helping me become the woman I am today."[8]
>
> —*Shadiya Manadath*

Humaira was shocked when one of his cousins got into a fight with her sister and stomped on the ground in anger. In India, it would be considered very rude to behave this way.

Many Indian immigrants and their children felt as though they lived in two cultures but were not wholly a part of either.

▲ **Some Hindus have a religious space inside their homes.**

▲ **Hindu worship can involve making offerings.**

On weekends, they went to the temple to worship and to learn traditional Indian dance and music. It was a space that was both Indian and American and, at the same time, neither.

The Hindu concept of **seva**, or service to the poor, was central to the experience of many Indian American families. Many Indian immigrants shared their good fortune by sending money to their families at home. They valued volunteering and supporting their neighbors, both in their new communities and the ones they had left behind.

Chapter 4

THE TECHNOLOGY BOOM

Harshini Bacchu stared at the beige-colored walls of her apartment. She sighed before getting the vacuum out and cleaning the carpet. Her new husband, Anjan, was at work at a temporary computer job in California. Anjan drove their only car. He often worked long hours.

◄ **Rosen Sharma has helped create many U.S. technology companies. He graduated from the Indian Institute of Technology Delhi in India before coming to the United States.**

Harshini watched the minutes tick by on the clock. She felt trapped at home day after long day.

When Anjan told her that he had lost his job, Harshini also had news for him. She was pregnant. She wanted the baby to be born in the United States so the child would be a U.S. citizen. If Anjan didn't find a new job right away, they could be forced to leave the country.

Anjan took Harshini to see New York City before the baby was born. They admired the Brooklyn Bridge, the Statue of Liberty, and the bright lights of Times Square. This was the America Harshini had always imagined. But when her daughter, Amita, was born, Harshini wanted to move back to India.

When Amita was one month old, Anjan drove his wife and daughter to the airport. He kissed the baby's forehead. Harshini cried on his shoulder. Anjan told her to eat well and take care of herself. She told him not to worry about them. As Anjan watched his wife wheel the stroller toward the airplane gate, he had second thoughts about his choice to be separated from his family. "I'm sad that now I'm lost in this world," he said.[9]

▲ Sometimes Indian immigrants move back to India so their children can learn about their culture.

Anjan was among 100,000 technology workers who came to the United States from India in the year 2000. The technology job market was booming. However, it would soon decline sharply. Many Indian immigrants faced a difficult choice. They had to decide whether it was worth staying in the United States or whether they should return to their families in India.

◀ Some Indian immigrants come to the United States to start a family.

25

Chapter 5

MODERN IMMIGRANTS

O n September 12, 2001, Sher Singh boarded a train from Boston, Massachusetts, to his home in Virginia. He was a Sikh, and he wore the traditional turban. It was the day after the September 11 terrorist attacks on the World Trade Center in New York City. Some people were suspicious of anyone who was Muslim or who they incorrectly believed looked Muslim.

This was unfair to many people. The vast majority of Muslims did not want to harm the United States.

Police boarded the train and pointed their rifles at Singh. Someone had thought Singh looked Muslim, but they didn't know the differences between Muslims and Sikhs. The police handcuffed Singh and dragged him off the train. A crowd gathered on the platform, chanting, "Kill him."[10] The police realized quickly Singh was innocent. Yet even after he was released, his picture was broadcast on television for days.

Singh had been a U.S. citizen since 1998. He had done nothing wrong. Yet he was not bitter about his arrest. "In situations where you go through some horrific events, it is possible to make an error in judgment," he said. "They felt they were doing the right thing."[11] However, it's not right to assume something about a person based on their race or religion.

As a result of his experience on the train, Singh and his wife decided it was important to increase tolerance and understanding among Americans. They dedicated themselves to educating others about the Sikh faith.

Many Indian immigrants worked hard to keep their traditions alive in the United States. They held **pujas**. They read Indian mythology to their children and held parties and gatherings.

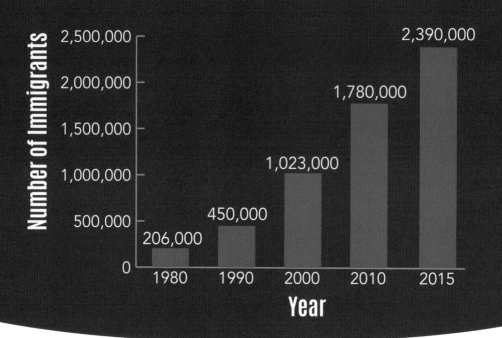

INDIAN IMMIGRANT POPULATION (1980-2015)

Number of Immigrants (vs.) Year

- 1980: 206,000
- 1990: 450,000
- 2000: 1,023,000
- 2010: 1,780,000
- 2015: 2,390,000

They celebrated Diwali, the Hindu New Year. Indian restaurants and Bollywood films became part of mainstream American life.

In 2018, the U.S. government made it harder for noncitizens to get work visas. It also began enforcing immigration laws more strictly. But millions of Indian Americans live in the United States and have achieved remarkable success. Many of them have college degrees. They also have the highest incomes compared with the general population in the United States.

Today's U.S. immigration system favors highly skilled and educated people. Therefore, many Indian Americans work as doctors and engineers. Some are CEOs of major companies such as Microsoft, Google, and Pepsi. Many also work as lawyers, judges, and politicians. Some Indian Americans have also been considered as justices for the Supreme Court.

However, not all Indian Americans enter the country with high levels of education or wealth. Some work long hours at convenience stores, gas stations, or motels. In time, many have worked their way up to managing or owning these businesses. Indian immigrants face different experiences when coming to the United States.

THINK ABOUT IT

- How do you think immigration of Indian citizens to the United States has both helped and hurt India?
- How is the concept of seva, or service, seen in other cultures or faiths?
- Do you think it's fair to judge people by how they look? Explain your answer.

GLOSSARY

caste (KAST): The caste system divides Hindus into strict social classes. The caste system limits the job and educational opportunities of many Indian people.

discrimination (diss-krim-in-AY-shun): Treating a person or group of people unfairly because of their race or gender is known as discrimination. Many Indian immigrants faced discrimination after the September 11, 2001, terrorist attacks.

pujas (POO-juhz): Pujas are Hindu prayer rituals. Many Indian immigrants perform pujas at altars in their homes.

quota (KWOH-tuh): A quota limits the number of people allowed to do something. The quota system that limited Indian immigrants ended in 1965.

sari (SAHR-ee): A sari is the traditional dress of Indian women. Many Indian American women continue to wear the traditional sari.

segregated (SEG-rih-gate-id): To be segregated is to be kept away or separate from another group. Indian immigrants faced hardships in the segregated South.

seva (SAY-va): Seva is the Hindu concept of service to others. Seva is an important part of Indian culture.

turmeric (TUR-mer-ik): Turmeric is a bright yellow spice grown in India. Turmeric is used in both Indian medicine and cooking.

visas (VEE-zuhz): Visas are documents or stamps that shows permission for a person to enter another country. Many immigrants receive visas that allow them to travel to the United States.

SOURCE NOTES

1. "My Name Is Roshan Sharma." *First Days Project*. South Asian American Digital Archive, n.d. Web. 3 Aug. 2018.

2. Erika Lee. "Legacies of the 1965 Immigration Act." *SAADA*. SAADA, 1 Oct. 2015. Web. 3 Aug. 2018.

3. "My Name Is B.P. Rao." *First Days Project*. South Asian American Digital Archive, n.d. Web. 3 Aug. 2018.

4. "My Name Is Basil Varkey." *First Days Project*. South Asian American Digital Archive, n.d. Web. 3 Aug. 2018.

5. Ibid.

6. "The Remarkable Story of How an Immigrant's Hunger Created the US's Biggest Indian Grocery Chain." *Quartz*. Quartz, 3 July 2017. Web. 3 Aug. 2018.

7. "My Name Is Sakti Kunz." *First Days Project*. South Asian American Digital Archive, n.d. Web. 3 Aug. 2018.

8. "My Name Is Shadiya Manadath." *First Days Project*. South Asian American Digital Archive, n.d. Web. 3 Aug. 2018.

9. "Anjan and Harshini Bacchu." *TPT*. Independent Television Service, n.d. Web. 3 Aug. 2018.

10. Valarie Kaur. "For Sikhs and Muslims, Fear after a Terror Attack." *Washington Post*. Washington Post Company, 23 Apr. 2013. Web. 3 Aug. 2018.

11. "9/11 Decade: Sher Singh Holds No Grudges 10 Years Later." *Sikh Philosophy Network*. Sikh Philosophy Network, 9 Sept. 2011. Web. 3 Aug. 2018.

TO LEARN MORE

Books

Bartell, Jim. *India*. Minneapolis, MN: Bellwether Media, 2011.

Blevins, Wiley. *India*. New York, NY: Children's Press, 2018.

Centore, Michael. *India*. Broomall, PA: Mason Crest, 2015.

Web Sites

Visit our Web site for links about Indian immigrants: childsworld.com/links

Note to Parents, Teachers, and Librarians: We routinely verify our Web links to make sure they are safe and active sites. So encourage your readers to check them out!

INDEX